With Love, The Itty-Bitty Calico Kitty™

Beth Freeman

Illustrations by Nik Henderson

ISBN: 978-1-7166-8899-7 (sc)
ISBN: 978-1-7165-4624-2 (hc)
ISBN: 978-1-7166-8370-1 (e)

Library of Congress Control Number: 2020915477

Lulu Publishing Services rev. date: 10/06/2020

This book belongs to:

_____

_____

_____

Dedicated to the memory of the
Itty-Bitty Calico Kitty and her beloved sister, Ellie.

Table of Contents

Lost and Found..1

Foster Home...5

Life in a Crate...9

Giving Love 13

Receiving Love 17

Finding My Forever Home 21

Home at Last!.. 25

Loving Like Cats and Dogs.. 29

Forever Love 33

Message of Love 36

Lost and Found

"I am lost and scared, but I know someone kind will find me and love me," thought the Itty-Bitty Calico Kitty.

Have you ever been lost?

It's okay to be scared sometimes.

Look for someone with kind eyes to help you. Kind people can be found and kind people will stick around!

Foster Home

"I know this isn't my real home, and it may not be my home for long, but I feel safe here." The Itty-Bitty Calico Kitty sighed.

Have you ever stayed somewhere that wasn't home?

It's okay to be away from home, away from anywhere, as long as you feel safe and sound and others are around!

Life in a Crate

"I know I'm not well enough to play with the other kittens," thought the Itty-Bitty Calico Kitty, "and I don't want the others to get sick and sad. I look forward to playing with them and being happy and glad."

Have you ever had to stay home because you were sick?

It's okay to feel lonely, and it's all right to feel left out when you're sick.

You can play again when you are all better, and then you can get into the thin and the thick!

Giving Love

"I am so thankful for those who are helping me. I'm going to give them all the love I can, all the love and all the glee." The Itty-Bitty Calico Kitty purred.

Have you ever been thankful for those who show you love?

It's okay to show your feelings and give love and laughter to those who love you!

Receiving Love

"I know that I deserve love." The Itty-Bitty Calico Kitty said. "So I am going to soak it all in and then some more and then again!"

Have you ever wondered why someone loves you?

Well, it's okay to wonder why and even who! You absolutely deserve love just for being you!

Finding My Forever Home

"I was a little shy at first with my new family, but then my new mommy was so soft and cuddly and my new doggy sister, Ellie, licked me right on the face. I felt so loved." The Itty Bitty Calico Kitty sighed.

Have you ever met someone new and felt a little shy?

It's okay to be a little nervous with new people, but if they are kind to you, then you can be kind too!

It feels really great, and it's the loving thing to do!

Home at Last!

"Love is what home feels like," thought the Itty-Bitty Calico Kitty. "Playtime and snuggle time all the time, I can be myself, I am loved, and I get to love too!"

Have you ever felt loved for just being you?

It's okay if you have, and it's okay if you have not because I'm here to tell you that I love you a lot! Just for being you!

Loving Like
Cats and Dogs

"A dog may love differently than a cat. Hmm. I have never thought about that, but dogs want to show love and feel love too," stated the Itty-Bitty Calico Kitty.

Have you ever noticed that you show your love differently from your sister or your brother or your daddy or your mother?

It's okay because no matter how they show it everyone wants love deep down inside. I know it.

So show your love the way you feel, and feel it all because it's real!

Forever Love

"I know I am sick and that I may not be here forever, but I've loved and I've been loved so much that I will never be forgotten," stated the Itty Bitty Calico Kitty.

Have you ever lost someone or something you loved?

It's okay to be sad. I want to share something important with you. Love never dies. No, it don't do! It just stays in your heart forever and ever and ever too!

"Love," the Itty Bitty Calico Kitty taught, "is meant to be shared!"

Give love and share love, and you will receive love. And most of all, you deserve love—no matter how big, no matter how small, no matter how short, no matter how tall, no matter how well, no matter how sick, you are deserving of love. You see, that is the trick!